ONCE UPON A DREAM

The Echoes Of Dreams

Edited By Lynsey Evans

First published in Great Britain in 2024 by:

YoungWriters Est. 1991

Young Writers
Remus House
Coltsfoot Drive
Peterborough
PE2 9BF
Telephone: 01733 890066
Website: www.youngwriters.co.uk

All Rights Reserved
Book Design by Ashley Janson
© Copyright Contributors 2024
Softback ISBN 978-1-83565-545-0
Printed and bound in the UK by BookPrintingUK
Website: www.bookprintinguk.com
YB0594Y

FOREWORD

Welcome Reader, to a world of dreams.

For Young Writers' latest competition, we asked our writers to dig deep into their imagination and create a poem that paints a picture of what they dream of, whether it's a make-believe world full of wonder or their aspirations for the future.

The result is this collection of fantastic poetic verse that covers a whole host of different topics. Let your mind fly away with the fairies to explore the sweet joy of candy lands, join in with a game of fantasy football, or you may even catch a glimpse of a unicorn or another mythical creature. Beware though, because even dreamland has dark corners, so you may turn a page and walk into a nightmare!

Whereas the majority of our writers chose to stick to a free verse style, others gave themselves the challenge of other techniques such as acrostics and rhyming couplets.

Each piece in this collection shows the writers' dedication and imagination – we truly believe that seeing their work in print gives them a well-deserved boost of pride, and inspires them to keep writing, so we hope to see more of their work in the future!

CONTENTS

Ashurst CE Aided Primary School, Ashurst

Millie Green (10)	1
Isla Humphreys (10)	2
Theo Sheldon (9)	3
Sienna Blomquist (9)	4
Octavia Peill (9)	5
Philippa Julian (9)	6
Mia Faust (9)	7
Odin Daly (8)	8
Emily Weekley (9)	9
Rose Topping (10)	10
Sophie Weekley (8)	11
Rose Maddock (10)	12
Aurelia Ghorishi Robinson (8)	13
Matteo Corsoni (9)	14
Ferdie Sowter (10)	15

Ballymagee Primary School, Bangor

Chloe Wilkinson (11)	16
Nathan King (9)	17
Imogen Compton (8)	18
Lena Hegarty (7)	19
Sophia McCready (9)	20
Victoria Gilmour (7)	21

Brambles Primary Academy, Brambles Farm

Faithful Oluwadare (11)	22
Adley McCann (11)	23
Ava Stevenson (10)	24
Dylan Welsh (11)	25

Brooklyn Paul (11)	26
Darcie Fitzsimmons (11)	27
Magnus Denedo (11)	28
Kain Elliott (11)	29
Peace Owolabi (10)	30
Penelope Strickland (10)	31
Ethan Patterson (10)	32
Praise Omo-Osawaru (11)	33
Lexie Reynolds (10)	34
Harrison McPhillips (10)	35
Caleb Wright (10)	36
Fletcher Willmott (11)	37
Lincoln Bryant (11)	38
Katie H (11)	39
Ella Obrien (11)	40
Hope Baikie (10)	41
Mason Hugill (10)	42
Jayden James (10)	43

Central Primary School, Watford

Jesse	44

Crossways Junior School, Thornbury

Charis Riddiford (9)	45
Sophie-Anne Seamark (10)	46
Ellie Tucker (9)	47
Margot Chavaroche Kumolka (9)	48
James Marmont (9)	49
Izzy Tucker (9)	50
Rihanna Barter (9)	51

Dreghorn Primary School, Dreghorn

Levi Forsyth (11)	52
Noah Shedden (11)	54
Bethany Watson (10)	56
Jack Armstrong (10)	58
Isla Gregory (10)	60
Lewis Mcintyre (11)	61
Maya Cousar (11)	62
Abbey Higgins (11)	63
Hollie Simpson (12)	64
Alfie Cushnaghan (10)	65
James Wilson (11)	66
Kayla McCluskey (11)	67
Evie Miller (10)	68
Emily Cameron (10)	69
Sophie Stevenson (10)	70
Ben Smith (11)	71
Poppy Mitchelhill (10)	72
Elise Cochrane (11)	73
Lucas Burns (10)	74

Forest Academy, Brandon

Blake Sutton (10)	75
Izabelle Bowe (10)	76
Liana Kiskenaite (10)	78
Brooke Nolder (9)	79
Amelia Sayer (10)	80

Hague Bar Primary School, New Mills

Beatrix Robinson (10)	81
Nina Reitze (11)	82
Noah Stillman-Cox (7)	84
Hazel Hopkins (7)	85
Grace Rudder (8)	86
Carys Botham (10)	87
Roy Kinnar Jnr (10)	88
Grace Edge (7)	89

Harborne Primary School, Harborne

Amina Junaid (11)	90
Hiranya Nukala (11)	92
Charlotte James (11)	93
Aya Agha (10)	94
Aarna Bhargava (11)	95
Soujanya Shanmugam (11)	96

Highcliffe St Mark Primary School, Highcliffe

Finlay Torrington (10)	97
Alba Mussell (9)	98
Erin Lowe (9)	100
Holly-Fay Middleton-Moore (10)	101
Bobby Blow (10)	102
Lexie Fidler (10)	103
Jasmine Jackson (10)	104
Lola Watson (10)	105
Imogen Pengelly (9)	106
Phoebe Holdsworth (9)	107
Jake Moxom (9)	108
Evie Bellamy (9)	109
Emily Edwards (9)	110
Grace Head (9)	111
Jake Waldron (9)	112
Lydia Pengelly (9)	113
Charlie Jarvis (9)	114
Henry Findlay (10)	115
Riley Parker-Tait (10)	116
Samuel Watts (10)	117
Megan Lammers (9)	118

Hormead CE School, Great Hormead

Joshua Millbrow (8)	119
Erin Laidler (8)	120
Niamh Hennessey (8)	121

James Cambell Primary School, Dagenham

Ben Skinsley (9)	122
Teagan Rema (9)	124
Ivan Al-Wakeel (10)	126
Gabi Dumitrescu (10)	127
Freya Ellis (10)	128
Aka Onuorah (10)	129
Mehroz Riaz (9)	130
Artiom Pozdirea (10)	131
Gabriele Stravinskaite (9)	132
Michelle Oloko (9)	133

Kirkinner Primary School, Kirkinner

Alfie Marr (10)	134
Lily McShane	135
Leyla McQueen (10)	136
Carter Hastie (10)	137
Georgie Doherty (8)	138

Lawn Primary School, Allestree

Jay Chauhan (8)	139

Parsloes Primary School, Dagenham

Shahmeen Jalil (8)	140
Fatima Zubair (9)	141
Daria Onila (9)	142
Ella Avram (9)	143
Owen Clavier (9)	144

Pencombe CE Primary School, Pencombe

Mabel Hatt (8)	145

Ramsbury Primary School, Ramsbury

Sophia Ashby (8)	146

Charlotte Pontoppidan-Toms (10)	148
Abi Fellows (9)	149
Lorcan Cooper (10)	150
Izzy Gray (8)	151
Alex Soper (8)	152
Iris Fawcus (9)	153

Rufford Primary & Nursery School, Bulwell

Khaleelah Gbagba (9)	154
Victor Adebayo (8)	155
Jayden Lewis (9)	156
Georgia Sail (9)	157
Jack Boardman (9)	158
Brayden Chadwick (8)	159

Sacred Heart RC Primary School, Birchfield

Henon Yosef (10)	160
Emmanuella Chinedu (10)	161
Tanjima Hassain (10)	162
Tavia Morgan (10)	163
Sarina Zegard (9)	164
Kha'mya Gayle	165
Raphael Glorified (10)	166
Oluwaferanmi Ayandiran (9)	167
Sarina Suha Zegard (10)	168

Sandcross School, Reigate

Seren Walker-Samuel (7)	169
Elizabeth Reeve (7)	170
Amelia Marsh (7)	173
Harry Rheinberg (8)	174
Connie Noble (8)	175

St James's RC Primary School, Twickenham

Kaila Kovalcik (10)	176
Matthew Zuaiter Viono (11)	178
Kylie Lo (11)	179

The Eveline Day School, Tooting

Anna Kostyleva (9)   180

THE POEMS

Nightmare Embers

Crackle, snap. Flames are right in my face, flaring and whirling in a deadly dance.
Screaming and shouting, I kick and scream, but I'm stuck in this spiralling trance.
Blazing flames whip my legs, burning and stabbing at my shoulders.
I run and run, but my feet are heavy, stomping just like boulders.
"Let go of me!" I try to scream, but my voice is muffled and quiet.
It engulfs my vision and I see my crying family, screaming like there's a riot.
I can't see anything, with tears welling up in my eyes.
I wake up screaming and crying, a feeling I despise.
Humiliation burns as I'm filled with woe.
It wasn't that scary, but my heart doesn't think so!

Millie Green (10)
Ashurst CE Aided Primary School, Ashurst

Nightmare Scare

It is finally night
No please don't turn off the light
Why my son, full of fear?
Because all the monsters will come here
She turns off the light
Then, there comes the big fright.

Black, scary spiders crawl around the walls
And behind me, there is a crowd of ghastly ghouls
There are emerald, scaly snakes surrounding the floor
I don't think I can do this, I'm fleeing out the door
I go to the bathroom, all I can see is smoke
Maybe it is all just a joke.

I run outside as fast as I could
It really should end, I wish it really would
But then I wake up with my mum next to me
Saying it was all just a bad dream.

Isla Humphreys (10)
Ashurst CE Aided Primary School, Ashurst

Dinosaur

Dinosaurs, dinosaurs,
Dinosaurs everywhere.
Some big, some small.
From air, to ground, to sea.
Fast to slow, I love dinos.
Big teeth, small teeth.
All of them unique.

They have bright eyes, that pierce the night.
Their footsteps echo in the darkness, left and right.
Underwater their roar is as loud as sixty hounds.
Knocking the tiny fish right to the ground!
They steal the other dinos' eggs out of the nests,
Always doing it at their best.
The flying dinos search the land,
While the small ones will try not to lose a hand.
I love dinos.

Theo Sheldon (9)
Ashurst CE Aided Primary School, Ashurst

Disappearing School

Down in the darkness where the moles sleep
My gazing eyes lay upon some sheep
It's a usual day, ready for seven o'clock
But something feels strange and where's my sock?
When I walk out the door with the future upon
My mouth is as wide as a gate, this was more than beyond.

I'm in the future, how strange is that?
And I see people with holographic cats
Then I realise, it's a school day
Oh no! I'll have to find my way
The school is nowhere to be seen
But all of this was just a dream.

Sienna Blomquist (9)
Ashurst CE Aided Primary School, Ashurst

A Fantasy Girl

I am a fantasy girl,
In a fantasy world,
With strawberry-laced hair,
Lollipop earrings, candyfloss skirts,
And a flowing, stripy, bubblegum shirt,
Why, oh why, does this dream have to stop?
Unicorns around go clipperty clop,
Bunnies go hop, hop, hop,
People are drinking fizzy pop,
Then suddenly, my eyes go blurry,
And I cannot see,
What is happening to me,
I close my eyes and count to ten,
I take a breath and open them,
Wow, this was all just a dream,
I tried not to scream.

Octavia Peill (9)
Ashurst CE Aided Primary School, Ashurst

Frog

I closed my eyes, waiting for dread,
I opened them again – was there something under my bed?
I heard barking – was it my dog?
I opened the door, and in hopped a frog!
Faster than an eel!
Bigger than a seal!
With green-emerald scales,
I was shocked to find three dog tails!
I raced down the stairs; it wasn't behind me,
I would have run faster if I'd known it was beside me,
I ran down the hallway, now only half the size,
Of the gigantic frog, whom I now despised!

Philippa Julian (9)
Ashurst CE Aided Primary School, Ashurst

The Dream Bus

Dreams start at the edge of the night
As soon as you turn off the light.
But there is one special dream about a bus,
No ordinary bus, no.
A flying bus with a girl and her two cats.

Whoosh!
And off it went.
Soaring through the sky,
Past the clouds,
Past the stars,
And past a cow jumping over the moon.

In the bus were jars of glowing dreams.
Ding ding,
There goes the alarm.
Phew,
It was all a dream!

Mia Faust (9)
Ashurst CE Aided Primary School, Ashurst

Sweet World

C hocolate is what I see everywhere around me
H ow lovely is this like being in a pool of chocolate
O h this is so lovely I see Willy Wonka that's what I see
C ould I eat all of this tree all the bark too
O r I could eat all the leaves
L ate, late I am for the feast
A ll the people have eaten their candy
T ea that is what I'm late for
E ating is so yummy.

Odin Daly (8)
Ashurst CE Aided Primary School, Ashurst

Run!

I run,
Run as fast as I can,
This is no fun,
Is this the plan?

A mass of fog surrounds me,
The twists and turns,
How can I flee?
It will destroy me.

I slip but fall,
It comes so close,
I feel so small,
I close my eyes.

The walls disappear,
The monster takes me,
It all becomes clear,
It was just a dream!

Emily Weekley (9)
Ashurst CE Aided Primary School, Ashurst

Help Me...

I wake up
What's on my wall?
It's a spider not big at all
Oh wait give me a shake
I hate them
Let's run into the sun.

I look back
Where is it?
It's bigger and blacker
It's a trap
I run in a maze
To a big clock
Then a beep is heard
I wake with a shake.

Rose Topping (10)
Ashurst CE Aided Primary School, Ashurst

Unicorns Disappeared

U nicorns soaring through the sky
N ine of them had disappeared!
I was so worried
C ould it be a monkey?
"**O** h yes," said a voice
"**R** un or it will be you next!"
"**N** o," I said loudly
S illy me it was just a dream, or was it?

Sophie Weekley (8)
Ashurst CE Aided Primary School, Ashurst

A Magical Past

A wizard took me to the past
Where dragons roamed the Earth and wizards and witches lived beside them
Unicorns running wildly through the woods
Sparkling waterfalls and streams gushing through the village
There were blackberry bushes growing all around me
Now I wake up with happy thoughts in my head.

Rose Maddock (10)
Ashurst CE Aided Primary School, Ashurst

The Monster Dash

Once upon a dream,
I was having a good time,
I looked behind me,
There was a monster,
I ran and ran, but that didn't help me,
I couldn't believe my eyes,
But I cried,
I got home and sat in my bed,
But in front of me the monster was there,
Was it a dream or was it real?

Aurelia Ghorishi Robinson (8)
Ashurst CE Aided Primary School, Ashurst

Sweety Lands Sweets

S weets are yummy
W atery jelly is in my tummy
E ating bigger to smaller chocolates
E ating sweets that are super
T alking candyfloss
S weets are the sugar boss

Matteo Corsoni (9)
Ashurst CE Aided Primary School, Ashurst

Avengers Assemble

M en meet to begin the fight
A man is down
R etreat to base
V ery bad people are there
E veryone is here
L ead to win.

Ferdie Sowter (10)
Ashurst CE Aided Primary School, Ashurst

Tonight's Dream

T onight's movie is gonna start!
O h, they're in the dark,
N o, don't go down there!
I t's a vicious bear!
G ood, it's gone now,
H ome, why is there a cardboard cow?
T o the barn, we go!
S tarting another movie.

D are to go in there, a lion's in it,
R accoons are in the bins!
E agles soaring through the night sky,
A nimals say bye,
M y dreams are really weird.

Chloe Wilkinson (11)
Ballymagee Primary School, Bangor

Moonbeams

My nights are without darkness.
I see the moonbeams shine through the floating majestic clouds.
The twirling stars catch the tails of those beautiful beams
As I sit upon my glittering star in awe of how wonderful this life I have is.
The pitch-blackness of the night is illuminated by the brightest of moons.
As I drift off to sleep I can see the moonbeams through my window and it makes me feel safe.
I cannot wait for nightfall again so that I can visit my moonbeam dreams.

Nathan King (9)
Ballymagee Primary School, Bangor

Chocolate Cheetah In Candyland

A land of sweets and marshmallow fights
Is what I dream about at night.
My toys and cat are all there
We play all night with no parents aware.
Cheetah is her name
My pet cat is so much fun.
She is insanely fast and agile, like a jet plane
With a beautiful chocolate-coloured mane.
Candyland is so much fun
It's a place for everyone.
Boys and girls, pets and toys
We always feel so much joy.

Imogen Compton (8)
Ballymagee Primary School, Bangor

Dragons

I dream about dragons on a faraway planet,
Wings flapping, they're about to land.
I take a step forward,
The dragon is friendly,
She bows her head.
Does she want me to ride her?
I know this is just a dream,
But I can't help but enjoy the thrill,
Of flying on a sapphire-blue dragon.
I wake up with a smile on my face,
I hope that planet is real.

Lena Hegarty (7)
Ballymagee Primary School, Bangor

Summer

Summer, summer is here!
Bright and warm
Sun shining beautiful
Kids playing all around
Ice cream everywhere
People having a blast screaming
Flowers blooming all around
Everyone loves summer!
Warm and beautiful
Eating ice lollies
Birds singing all around
Parks full, swings full!
People are having parties.

Sophia McCready (9)
Ballymagee Primary School, Bangor

Rainbow Fairies

F luttering fairies flying by.
A lways careful where they fly.
I ncreasing their speed as they race through the skies.
R ainbows appear while fairies dance by.
I s this rainbow going to go so high?
E veryone loves this fairyland.
S haring love all around.

Victoria Gilmour (7)
Ballymagee Primary School, Bangor

Door Of Dreams

If I were a dark red door,
I would show you the puppy of
Falling blood, and burning lava rising
From the ground.

If I were a royal blue door,
I would take you to a paradise of
Crystal-clear skins, sparkling blue dolphins, perfect
Macau and the lost city of Atlantis.

If I were a brown door, I would take you
The way of a warrior and give you the power
To destroy one thousand enemies.

If I were an amber door, I would give you
Years of age, gallons of honey and bright daylight.

If I were a green door,
I would stop you from getting hurt,
And help you when you were tired,
And make you happy every day.

Faithful Oluwadare (11)
Brambles Primary Academy, Brambles Farm

Door Of Dreams

If I were a blood-red door,
I would show you,
The danger of the underworld,
A deep river of blood,
And a world of brutal imposters.

If I were a sky-blue door,
I would take you,
To a paradise full of beautiful butterflies,
A world of calmness,
Or a crystal-clear ocean of dreams.

If I were a pitch-black door,
I would stop you,
From entering a life filled with disaster,
A world full of evilness,
Or a sinister, treacherous end.

If I were a rose-pink door,
I would teach you,
To climb the tallest mountain,
Make the most perfect rose,
Or take you to a land,
Carpeted with flowers.

Adley McCann (11)
Brambles Primary Academy, Brambles Farm

The Dreams Of A Pale Cherry-Pink Door

If you open the pale, cherry-pink door,
You will be taken away to a majestic land of dreams and hope,
First, we see a beach,
With the most pretty, pale, cherry-pink sand,
With a glowy, pink sea.
Then, you will see,
The biggest sakura trees,
In the midnight skies.
Once we go past the pink lake,
You will see a beautiful mermaid,
Lying on the sand,
With cherry-pink hair,
And a pale, pink tail,
And we will pass through the field of cherry blossoms,
In the sunset,
Then, we will be at a cake show,
And they will do pink cakes.

Ava Stevenson (10)
Brambles Primary Academy, Brambles Farm

Door Of Dreams

If I were a deep red door,
I would show you the entrance to death,
In a room full of bloodstained walls,
Or an ancient abandoned territory,
Overflowing with skeletons.

If I were a crystal-clear door,
I would take you
To a world of dolphins,
A place of the relaxing sea,
Or an aquarium full of fascinating
marine creatures.

If I were a black, haunted door,
I would teach you
The basics of evilness,
The secrets of the afterlife,
Or the sinister wickedness of
the possessed realm.

Dylan Welsh (11)
Brambles Primary Academy, Brambles Farm

If I Were…

If I were a fancy green door,
I would take you to
A place full of luscious grass,
A great place filled with all trees,
Or a land rich with flowers everywhere.

If I were a blood-red door,
I would take you to
A lake full of bubbling blood,
A land with Chinese lanterns,
Or a vine of big, juicy tomatoes.

If I were a navy blue door,
I would teleport you to
A battlefield of danger,
A field full of blueberries,
Or a large swimming pool filled with dolphins.

Brooklyn Paul (11)
Brambles Primary Academy, Brambles Farm

Door Of Dreams

If I were a scarlet-red door,
I would show you
A deep, simmering volcano.
A river filling with rubies,
Or a field full of black widow spiders.

If I were a royal blue door,
I would take you,
To sparkling sapphire caves,
To oceans with blue dolphins,
Or open land filled with iris or cornflowers.

If I were a violet-purple door,
I would teach you,
About the glory of amethysts,
The beauty of English lavender,
Or teach you about lilac flowers.

Darcie Fitzsimmons (11)
Brambles Primary Academy, Brambles Farm

If I Were A...

If I were a baby-blue door,
I would take you to a breathtaking, clear blue sky,
A stream of sparkling waters
Or a mythical forest with dragons.

If I were a pale green door,
I would take you to a beautiful filled forest,
A marvellous treehouse held by vines,
Or a wonderful flower-filled garden.

If I were a blood-red door,
I would take you to
A battle with blood soldiers,
A blazing fire uphill,
Or a land filled with exploding volcanoes.

Magnus Denedo (11)
Brambles Primary Academy, Brambles Farm

Door Of Dreams

If I were a dark red door,
I would show you
A world filled with joy,
A life of sacrifice,
Or a river full of nightmares to remember.

If I were a crystal-blue door,
I would give you a life of paradise,
A world of exotic blue whales,
A crystal-clear sea to relax,
And a gleaming blue, cloudless sky.

If I were a ginger-orange door,
I would take you to a world of brightness,
A city full of inferno,
Or a moon of sleeping tigers.

Kain Elliott (11)
Brambles Primary Academy, Brambles Farm

The Dream Behind The Door

If I were a pink door,
I would lead you to a forest of enchanting cherry blossom,
I would take you through a garden of pink roses,
I would gift you a hot pink sapphire ring.

If I were a pink door,
I would gift you a bubblegum-pink diamond necklace,
I would take you to a pink sunset on the beach,
I would gift you a lake of luminescent
Pink mermaids, diving in and out of the waters.

Pink is love and care,
Pink is fair.

Peace Owolabi (10)
Brambles Primary Academy, Brambles Farm

Door Of Dreams

If I were a ruby-red door,
I would show you
A day full of happiness,
A sea full of joy and love,
Or a beautiful field filled with roses and poppies.

If I were a navy blue door,
I would take you
To see a blue whale,
To a relaxing ocean spa,
Or a fun-filled day of bluebirds and butterflies.

If I were an amethyst door,
I would teach you to help the poor,
To heal the hurt,
Or how to fight against evil.

Penelope Strickland (10)
Brambles Primary Academy, Brambles Farm

Door Of Dreams

If I were a blood-red door,
I would tell you
About the treacherous blood riser
Of a burning forest,
Of the devil himself.

If I were a crystal-clear blue door,
I would take you
To a sunken shipwreck,
A paradise of peacocks,
Or a cave of diamonds.

If I were an emerald-green door,
I would take you
To a grassland full of joy,
An enchanted forest walk,
Or a farm of grazing sheep.

Ethan Patterson (10)
Brambles Primary Academy, Brambles Farm

Door Of Dreams

If I were a danger door,
I would show you,
An ocean of red-hot lava,
An inflamed land full of red blood,
And a tower full of sinister and evil.

If I were a navy door,
I would take you,
To a land of blue skies and butterflies,
A mountain with crystal-clear waters,
Or an aquamarine full of dolphins and whales.

If I were a verdant green door,
I would teach you,
The way of lime and leafy sage,
To have the touch of emerald,
And to live a pastoral life.

Praise Omo-Osawaru (11)
Brambles Primary Academy, Brambles Farm

The Dream Behind The Door

If you open my turquoise-blue door,
I will take to to a clear blue beach,
Full of shiny crystals,
A tropical jungle,
Full of sapphire-blue leaves,
A giant ocean filled with arctic-blue jellyfish,
The middle of the North Pole,
To see aurora-blue Northern Lights,
A field full of morning glory flowers,
With delicate sky-blue butterflies,
And iridescent Oppenheimer Blue Diamonds,
Swirling at you.

Lexie Reynolds (10)
Brambles Primary Academy, Brambles Farm

If I Were A...

If I were a blood-red door,
I would take you to
A big field of poppies,
A place that's full of strawberries,
Or a big city of Chinese lanterns.

If I were a dark green door,
I would take you to
A place full of growing trees,
A vineyard full of growing grapes,
Or a beautiful busy rainforest.

Harrison McPhillips (10)
Brambles Primary Academy, Brambles Farm

The White Door

If I were a white door,
I would show you the white snow,
Then, I would show you,
The icy Atlantic floating on the ocean,
After that, I would take you,
Up to an azure-blue sky,
To see the fluffy clouds,
After that, I would take you to Alaska,
Where the Arctic foxes frolic,
In the freshly fallen snow.

Caleb Wright (10)
Brambles Primary Academy, Brambles Farm

If I Were…

If I were a blood-red door,
I would take you to
A garden of bright strawberries,
A land of Chinese lanterns
Or a place filled with mysterious things.

If I were a navy blue door,
I would take you to
A deep ocean to explore,
A big field of flowers
Or a sky garden full of fresh berries.

Fletcher Willmott (11)
Brambles Primary Academy, Brambles Farm

If I Were

If I were a deep red door,
I would teleport you to
A fire-breathing dragon,
A volcano of lava
Or a Chinese lantern world of happiness.

If I were a navy blue door,
I would transfer you to
A sea world of sharks and fish,
A crystal pool of dolphins
Or the Pacific Ocean to see whales.

Lincoln Bryant (11)
Brambles Primary Academy, Brambles Farm

The Dream Behind The Door

Open the door
You will find
The deep blue sea
As blue as the sky
The bright blue diamond
As true as the Aegean Sea
The lapis-blue stone
As blue as the marina.

Katie H (11)
Brambles Primary Academy, Brambles Farm

If I Were...

If I were a green, magic door,
I would teleport you,
To a place where sloths can crawl up trees,
A land where grasshoppers talk,
Or a rainforest surrounded by vines.

Ella Obrien (11)
Brambles Primary Academy, Brambles Farm

If I Were...

If I were a glittery, golden door,
I would take you to,
The Golden Gate of Heaven,
A place where angels play harps,
Or a place where puppies have magic wings.

Hope Baikie (10)
Brambles Primary Academy, Brambles Farm

If I Were...

If I were a baby-blue door,
I would take you to
A vast, beautiful sky view,
A gleaming land of sapphires
Or swimming in the most clear, deep waters.

Mason Hugill (10)
Brambles Primary Academy, Brambles Farm

If I Were...

If I were a sparkling red door,
I would show you a glamorous ruby world,
A big room with carmine stones,
Or a land where macaws fly around trees.

Jayden James (10)
Brambles Primary Academy, Brambles Farm

Football

Stars shine bright in the night like a diamond,
Cars smooth drive along the roads,
Giving me ages to look high in the sky as I drive by.
At night when the clouds appear,
My dreams are near.
Football is my dream,
Man City is my team.

Jesse
Central Primary School, Watford

Discover The Stars

One day I discovered the stars,
I discovered the sky,
While the gentlest of breezes swiftly passed me by,
I stumbled off of my scooter,
Fell down to my knees,
Then looked up and said, "Mum, what are these?"
"Well, they're called stars and that's called the sky."
I stopped and I stared,
I couldn't help but ask, "Why?"
"It's quite confusing and we'd better get home.
We're better off warm than hungry and cold."
That was the day I discovered the stars,
Next, guess what... I'll learn about Mars.

Charis Riddiford (9)
Crossways Junior School, Thornbury

Ballerinas

B allerinas twirl on the sparkling stage.
A s I stare, I start to feel amazed.
L ooking around the theatre, I see no other soul,
L ooking around the theatre, I start to take control.
E verywhere I peer, I see dancers disappear,
R unning daintily as can be.
I 'm swept onto the stage, velvet curtains surround me.
N ausea floods through my tummy, but...
A we-inspiringly, I begin to dance in front of the crowd, feeling light as a cloud.
S uddenly, I wake up to find my dad is snoring loud!

Sophie-Anne Seamark (10)
Crossways Junior School, Thornbury

When I Grow Up

Once upon a dream,
I dreamed that I was teaching the class.
I had a thought,
Should I be an astronaut,
Where I go up to space and discover planets?
Or a scientist who deals with chemicals and does experiments?
Or should I be a footballer,
Who scores goals and tackles people?
Or should I be a chef instead,
So I can cook food to feed the hungry?
Or a comedian who makes people laugh out loud?
But then I wake up in my bed,
And I realise it was all in my head.

Ellie Tucker (9)
Crossways Junior School, Thornbury

My Little Dream!

I stare, I glare from sun to moon,
I cuddle up with my witch sisters and our kittens.
They purr and mew from sun to noon,
And we dream away to the land of dreams.
I stare at the stars, then at my paws,
We climb on trees of an ancient forest.
The land changes and we are on the lovely roofs of Paris!
I was right since I was one!
The magic of dreams had been in me for years,
The wind rustles my chestnut fur,
I look at the girls
I love their cat forms!

Margot Chavaroche Kumolka (9)
Crossways Junior School, Thornbury

Dragons

D erek the dragon, the one who breathes fire,
R oderick the ruthless, the one who's aged higher,
A lex and Adam, the ones who eat mint,
G ruesome and Gross, they made a great glint,
O liver's oats make him thrive,
N utritious substances make us jive.
S o now you know what dragons do, it's time to learn about ghosts, boo!

James Marmont (9)
Crossways Junior School, Thornbury

My Whale

As I lie in my bed fast asleep
I enter the glittering sea
To find my whale waiting for me
It leaps up from deep in the darkest depths
And takes me down low on the seabed
We bob up and down around the globe
Sailing around by the cove
Until the moment's over, we laugh and laugh
And then I wake up, joy in my head

Izzy Tucker (9)
Crossways Junior School, Thornbury

Happy Dreams

H appening in front of my eyes all night,
A ppealing astronauts jumping and dancing,
P erfect cloud puppies chasing balls, so cute!
P ansies cover the field, I dance around in them,
Y ou lean over me and wake me up. It was all my imagination!

Rihanna Barter (9)
Crossways Junior School, Thornbury

Before The End Of My Dreams...

Every night before I go to bed, all my questions are left unread
As I start to doze off that is when my stories start to unfold
My eyes... open begging for air
Wandering around if there was no one else there
Smoke started to sprint down my throat, slowly disintegrating my big furry coat.
I was looking around this devastating sight
As something popped out, giving me a big fright!
The thing spun in circles, destroying everything in its path,
"Stop! Stop!" I burst out shouting, the thing looked up
And stopped moving.
My voice echoed around the destructive place,
While I watched acids fall, producing a big ugly face.
The ugly face spoke, "Who dares enter this nightmare scrap?
Thou must run before they fall into my trap!"
Before I could respond I heard a crash!
A big boulder dropped crashing and breaking until it came to a very quick stop.

I heard screaming and crying before the ground decided to swallow me whole.
I woke up in a nice happy place,
Planets floating as if I was in outer space.
Birds started to chirp, I felt like I was home.
I watched clouds fall producing a nice warm atmosphere.
Frogs hopped as cheetahs ran,
When all of a sudden wind rapidly blew like a big fan.
"I love it here," I shouted with joy,
When I finally woke up feeling dead coy.

Levi Forsyth (11)
Dreghorn Primary School, Dreghorn

My Classical Nightmare

As I rest my head on my pillow,
The slight sound of Mozart playing next to my bed,
I start to fall asleep, hoping for a good dream,
But what lies ahead will lead to even more trauma and anxiety.

A silky smooth carpet with a large painting on the wall,
Of a firm-looking man with a giant well-kept beard.
Hard marble and sandstone walls with a creaky wood floor
And giant antique music plays, producing a popular tune.

As I walk further into the house,
Lonesome sounds keep getting louder,
I feel almost watched by an outsider.
Thud! Creak! Creak! Creak! Creak!
It's behind me at the door,
A shadowy figure with great big roar,
Lurking in the darkness, it appears.

What was that lurking behind the door?
Why am I here?
As I walk ever further, a small cellar as cold as ice,
The steps I take on the stairs echo in my fear.

Suddenly, a roaring man with a manic grin on his face,
Comes sprinting with grey classic hair and a short beard.

As he starts to chase behind, my thoughts just rewind,
I wake up with sweat dropping down my face,
And a shiver shimmers down my spine.

Noah Shedden (11)
Dreghorn Primary School, Dreghorn

Delightful Dreams Waiting For Me

D reams wanting to be heard.
E veryone staring at me as I gaze into my delightful dream.
L ooking into my dream, hoping it would never end.
I gnoring the fact that I was literally tired in my dreams.
G azing over the lake of lilies as the cotton candy clouds towered over me.
H orrible thoughts leave my head as I fall right into bed.
T errific fun just waiting on me to share with my friends.
F ighting the urge to break free, what if I forget about this important dream?
U gly things leave my mind and go to the place of the unkind.
L ovely things that I cannot believe, will I ever come back?

D o you want to come here?
R oaring teddies saying, "Hug me, hug me!"
E agles soaring high in the sky.
A m I going to play with Bonny the Bubbly Bear ever again?
M um might worry, should I go?
S o, that's the end, goodbye!

Bethany Watson (10)
Dreghorn Primary School, Dreghorn

The Medieval Town

Once upon a dream
I suddenly appear in a medieval town
Where can I possibly be?
I see a man walk out of a bar
As I blink he walks out of my vision
I shout to see if anyone is near me
I walk around exploring

Suddenly I see a big, mysterious monster that appears out of the ground
I turn and sprint
The ground shakes as I run
I run into the bar and he's gone
W-what just happened?
I whimper, I'm scared

I look around and the man jumps up behind the counter
He says the world is ending
I run away in fear
I don't believe him
But the bar demolishes
I feel worried and scared

A couple more buildings demolish
A couple of minutes later they all disappear

I see a well
I go over and get some water
I need to find food
Oh, a stall
There's some apples and more!

Jack Armstrong (10)
Dreghorn Primary School, Dreghorn

Mystical Madness

In the land of my dreams,
I was shocked because this is what I could see.

Luscious green grass,
Unicorns flew like little sparks of colour and joy
As they raced through the sky.
A feeling of exhilaration as I watched a dragon breathe.
He breathed out love and wonder;
It filled me with wishes for what the future could be.

Fairies flew by, shimmering with shivers
As a gnarly gnome snarled with fury by the glistening river.
Gumdrops fell down; I caught one in my mouth.
My taste buds tingled as clouds of cotton candy fell down.

I was about to leave the land of my dreams,
But a leprechaun winked at me.
He placed a four-leaf clover in my hand
And started to do an adrenaline-filled dance.
I gave him a hug and waved goodbye.
I woke up in my bed, wishing I could go back sometime.

Isla Gregory (10)
Dreghorn Primary School, Dreghorn

Dream Rhyming Poem

When I went to sleep in my race car bed,
I found myself next to Ted.
He looked at me with fear and disgust,
then I knew I couldn't trust.

In a mystical lake in the sea,
I saw a stunning sunset next to me.
I blinked my eyes and felt the ground,
But this, I want to be around.

Somewhere in a grumpy galaxy far away,
I saw a gracious ghost that needs to lay,
At a relaxed restaurant where I want to stay.

At a waterfall full of wonders,
I saw a pirate ship that I wanted to plunder,
But what if I blunder?

Then I woke up in my hilarious house,
But then I saw a mouse,
And mice are my biggest fear.
But then my mum said, "It's okay, dear."

Lewis Mcintyre (11)
Dreghorn Primary School, Dreghorn

My Ocean Dreams

As I take a swim in the deep, in the deep Pacific Ocean,
I find myself floating further into the ocean.
I dive under the water as I rush myself through the coral,
The bright coral glows like a lamp.
The ocean's silent except for the distant bubbling.

Deeper under the water I encounter one of the ocean's giants,
A wonderful mind-warping whale shark,
Its stunning bright blue skin glows as it gets closer.
The whale shark is as big as a bus,
It glides over to me as I pat its fin.

As we go deeper into the sea,
The whale shark glides aside of me.
I have to wiggle as I float,
Out of my dream and back to the surface.

Maya Cousar (11)
Dreghorn Primary School, Dreghorn

The Dream That No One Else Would Dream

As I went to bed and closed my eyes,
I had a dream while snug and tight.
This kind of dream would leave you shocked,
And telling people might get you mocked.
In this dream, there's lots of colour,
Some colours are plain, but some may shimmer.
In this dream you may fly,
On the back of an animal, way up high.
In this dream, the grass is soft,
But the pollen in the air might make you cough.
In this dream the wind is light,
Giving you so much more delight.
As I opened up my eyes again,
I can see the beautiful sunrise again, as I say to myself,
"What a beautiful dream I had last night!"

Abbey Higgins (11)
Dreghorn Primary School, Dreghorn

The Bora Bora Dream

As my eyes slowly began to open wide,
I turned around and looked to my side.
Suddenly, I began to panic,
"Where on earth am I?"
I quickly jumped up and took a step outside.

As I hesitantly walked, I was shocked.
As I glanced, I noticed tall, gracious palm trees,
The crystal-clear aqua water and the sky,
With nothing but the gleaming sun.
My dream had come true, I was in Bora Bora!

But all alone, with no way to phone home,
With no one in sight, I began to shiver with fright.
Will I ever make it home, or will I forever be here, all alone?

Hollie Simpson (12)
Dreghorn Primary School, Dreghorn

The Cave Of Death

Night is the scariest time of the day,
Today I fell into a cave.
In the cave there was a bear,
As scary as my mum.

Geremy, yes, with a 'g', was the name of a dog
I found, he died later on but he was still cool.
"Have a share of depression," said the bear,
It died too.

The reason why they all died was toxic gas,
Mother Bear came and the toxic gas killed her too.
After everyone died, I died too.
Re-creation is what happened, now I'm a giraffe.

Everyone was fine,
No animals were harmed in the making of this poem.

Alfie Cushnaghan (10)
Dreghorn Primary School, Dreghorn

The Dream

In my neurological nightmare of fun, I noticed
A wicked witch winning a wager whilst wasting away
A demonic dog delivering a drink to a drunk doll
A teal taxi taking a tartan top hat to a party

In my neurological nightmare I summoned
A single sock spying on a stolen SIM card
A holy herd of henchmen hugging a hill
An incognito ibis on an incredible icicle

In my neurological nightmare of fun, I captured
A contaminated chicken cackling on a cream-coloured car
A rugged raptor ranting on a reinforced rainforest
A friendly French fry filled with fury

James Wilson (11)
Dreghorn Primary School, Dreghorn

The New York Nightmare

N ew York is where the nightmare starts, scared?
I 'm flying around New York when the ground looks close
G iant buildings all around when, *boom*, I hit the floor
H urts everywhere, when all of a sudden I can't see
T ombstone is near, I think, then I realise I'm moving
M an, help me! I'm starting to drift off, is this the end?
A rms and legs are weak. I'm struggling to breathe
R ight, this is the road. Wait, is that...
E erie endless dream, I thought as I slowly woke up.

Kayla McCluskey (11)
Dreghorn Primary School, Dreghorn

The Dragon Nightmare

Now, where the heck am I?
I'm in a broken castle,
Not a single soul in sight.
Glance around the room at the ivy-covered walls.
How did I end up here, in this horrid, disgusting place?
Thud. What was that?
A big shadow's on the wall.
My goodness, a dragon with a huge, slobbery jaw.
And it's getting closer!
What do I do?
Where do I go?
Run, run! Oh no, a dead end up ahead!
Everything's quiet.
Wait, I'm safe and sound in my bed.
Bye-bye, big dragon!
I'll see you again.

Evie Miller (10)
Dreghorn Primary School, Dreghorn

The Showjumping Dream

I walk into the ring, I see the prettiest jumps
My horse's hooves are as shiny as glittery gold
Nice new saddle pad from LeMieux

Oh no, it's my turn next
My hands begin to shake
Beat that, Emily, yes I will
The crowd scream with enjoyment, here we go!

First jump clear, the jumps screamed
As I jumped so high in the blue sky
Water jump now, splish splash,
I definitely didn't jump that like a coward

Clear round! Woohoo, I beat you, Bethany
The winner is Emily!

Emily Cameron (10)
Dreghorn Primary School, Dreghorn

Once Upon A Nightmare

N ever go in a maze at night
I f you do you'll get a fright
G o in you will see the devils chasing you and me
H and in hand I walked with Bethany and Poppy collectively feeling scared
T owers of treasures all around make sure to fix your frown
M ake sure you don't scream because the devils you may see
A ny money you may leave having fun will make you sneeze
R un away and never come back
E very night the wolves will attack.

Sophie Stevenson (10)
Dreghorn Primary School, Dreghorn

The Sun Bus

S oaring sun buses scatter through space,
U nusual animals living on stars,
N othing in sight but flying cars,

B eautiful bamboozled baboons on the moon,
U nder the bus is where you'll meet your doom,
S limy black fuel dripping from pipes, you'd better be careful of the spikes.

Ben Smith (11)
Dreghorn Primary School, Dreghorn

Once Upon A Dream

As I paddled my way through the glimmering lake
I felt the cold refreshing water soak into my skin
I heard nature's songs fill the fresh air
At the edge of the lake, I saw a group of turtles
Happily splashing in the bright shallow water
As the trees danced cheerfully in the glittering golden sun

Poppy Mitchelhill (10)
Dreghorn Primary School, Dreghorn

Once Upon A Disney World Dream

D elightful laughter from everywhere around,
R ides ready to welcome people on.
E xcellent rides in every corner of your eye,
A mazing adventures all around.
M illions of marvellous memories made,
S illy faces, whilst having a good time.

Elise Cochrane (11)
Dreghorn Primary School, Dreghorn

Once Upon A Dream

D oing five hundred keepie-uppies
R onaldo swapping shirts with me!
E xcellent overhead kicks
A mazing dribbles
M essi says I'm the best!

Lucas Burns (10)
Dreghorn Primary School, Dreghorn

The Weird Summer

It's snowing all summer,
Everyone eats ice cream in a block of ice,
Every time you pick up a book, it explodes,
The air smells like chocolate,
Everyone eats ice,
Jordan's are £1,
All video games are free,
Every dog has a hot dog body,
Pasta is the most popular food,
The end of the world happens,
Everyone has one town each,
There is a fun school in every town,
Every joke is funny,
Every step is 10k steps,
You walk 100k,
Free pizza for every peasant, man, woman and baddy,
Every question is wrong,
All people are invincible.

Blake Sutton (10)
Forest Academy, Brandon

Dream Doors

I open it wide,
And then peer inside,
To grin and shout in glee.
For the wonderful sight,
A dragon it might
Appear to be to me.

I step on through
And the dragon, it knew,
That all I would like is to fly.
It bows low to the ground,
Makes a growling sound,
And we set off into a violet sky.

We drift up in a cloud
And I hear a loud
Clip-clop of a nearby unicorn.
Floating near me
And buzzing like a bee,
Are phoenixes, newly born.

The dragon flies away,
And to music, we sway,
It takes me to where Hydras wallow.
Soon I say bye
And I, alone, fly,
Off in the land of mist and shadow.

Izabelle Bowe (10)
Forest Academy, Brandon

The Dreams

The sun was ready for a midnight nap,
The darkness woke up,
The children would fall asleep as quick as lightning,
The imagination fizzed and popped,
As sugarplums were dancing in their heads,
But some weren't flying horses and cute dogs,
But there were creepy monsters,
And they would see scenes of murder,
But they snap out of their heads and...
They would find them in their fluffy bed!

Liana Kiskenaite (10)
Forest Academy, Brandon

Dancing Pandas

Pandas like to dance,
The foxtrot, waltz and tango,
On the bus, train or plane,
On the way to Glasgow,
They dance in pairs or solo
While they like to take a photo.
Some are good, some are bad,
But no matter what, they are always glad.
When they arrive they have to pause,
Taking a bow for the excited applause.

Brooke Nolder (9)
Forest Academy, Brandon

Mystic Mystery

In the black sky and the moonlight, I try to find the sea tonight.
I travel around the world with Blaze (horse) making the night seem like day.
We finally find the deep blue sea,
Where a moonlight pony comes across to find me on the cliff up high.
As we find each other at the sea, we gallop up the ocean happily.

Amelia Sayer (10)
Forest Academy, Brandon

Scary Dream

Last night I had a scary dream,
The type where I wanted to scream,
I was walking on a pirate ship,
But then I began to slip.
My sword flew out of my hand,
"Who's there? Answer!" They command.
I quickly scrambled to my feet,
The tension grew, and it turned up the heat.
"It is I and I demand a duel!"
"Ha ha, shiver me timbers, you think you're cool,
I'm the best pirate throughout the land,
You think you can beat me? Maybe on sand."
Out from the shadows, the captain came out,
He was the scariest man I'd ever seen, without a doubt,
We grabbed our swords and marched onwards.
"Good luck," he whispered.
As we began to fight, I started out strong,
Midnight, and the clock went *dong*,
Until I lost and fell off the plank,
And down into the sky.
I woke up with a start,
Until I realised it was all a lie.

Beatrix Robinson (10)
Hague Bar Primary School, New Mills

A Vision

Up, up, in the sky above,
With wings white like a dove,
Down far below me,
I can see...
A thousand million things,
Birds floating on their wings,
Deserts wide and far,
And smoke coming from a car,
Coughing and choking me,
So I fly higher to be free,
Now below is a jungle scene,
So beautiful, a sea of green,
But the jungle is getting smaller,
Being cut down by a bulldozer,
I fly onto a land of snow,
But the ice is melting far below,
Turning around, left and right,
I try to escape this horrible sight,
And then on the sea so blue,
I see a turtle, in need of rescue,
He's trapped in a fishing net,
And to him, that's a big threat,

I wish I could stop it all,
But I can't move at all,
It's like I'm running through treacle,
Then I wake up and realise it's real,
Now every day I feel,
Like I'm still running through treacle,
Because I want to change things,
But I don't know how.

Nina Reitze (11)
Hague Bar Primary School, New Mills

The Witching Hour

T he horrible cackle of plotting witches in the sky
H orrifying goblins steal your gold and you scream until you die
E very monster comes out in the Witching Hour

W hen ghastly ghosts come up from their graves
I rritating bats come out from their caves
T he undead suck your blood
C raving demons take off their hoods
H aunting vampires never make a sound
I cy monsters stamp on the ground
N umb people try to get away
G raveyard devils make them stay

H eadless zombies gobble your brains
O ur hearts feel great pain
U tterly horrid, nasty ghouls
R evolting, snarling werewolves.

Noah Stillman-Cox (7)
Hague Bar Primary School, New Mills

Imagination

I n the deep and the darkness
M agic appears
A ntelopes dancing with very long beards
G raceful unicorns with soft, silky fur
I mps with their frightfully dangerous purr
N ever go near a bright, scary light
A screech of a witch, you must hold on tight
T ill then on, don't go too far
I t might not be great in the light of a star
O ccasionally, you could get stuck in glue
N ever have I seen them, but have you?

Hazel Hopkins (7)
Hague Bar Primary School, New Mills

The Princess' Crown

Twirling around like beautiful flowers
The princesses danced all night
One twirled around and lost her crown and she wondered what to do!
She searched high and low, left and right all through the night!
The king and queen heard her screams and said, "It'll be alright."
They sent her to bed, as she laid her head, she spotted it on her peg!

Grace Rudder (8)
Hague Bar Primary School, New Mills

At Night...

Once upon a dream at night,
Tucked up in bed so tight,
I dream of things great and small,
I dream of things tiny and tall,
I dream of things big and vast,
I dream of things from present and past.
All the things you could imagine in one place,
From the Earth to the moon to outer space!

Carys Botham (10)
Hague Bar Primary School, New Mills

Ice Field

A ten-day-long field of moving ice
Creaking and cracking ice drifting there, the sea
Bitter cold winds ripping there and towards her crew
A giant scaly maze of ice
A scaly and deserted landscape
As big as the humpback whales that live there

Roy Kinnar Jnr (10)
Hague Bar Primary School, New Mills

Llama Drama

Once my llama did some drama
In Rama, it had a friend called Tara
She was rather calmer
She sold her llama
Then the llama never did drama
Or talk to Tara
She just sat and relaxed and was calmer.

Grace Edge (7)
Hague Bar Primary School, New Mills

The Darkest Hour Is Just Before Dawn

I'm in my bed on a snowy night,
My eyes droop downwards, then I see a light,
I'm on a path as cold as snow,
The air as warm as the sun's glow,
This place is as beautiful as can be,
And I can see this new world all around me.

I walk further into this place,
And hear a sound along the glimmering path,
I turn towards it, only to face,
A monster about to unleash its wrath.

Light is sucked out of the air,
And the monster gives me a spine-chilling glare,
I wish I could hide; I wish I could run,
Away from the sight of anyone.

Then I begin to fall,
There is no bottom,
Not at all,
Suddenly, I'm in my bed,
My great relief cannot be said,

A moral from this story will spawn,
That the darkest hour is just before dawn.

Amina Junaid (11)
Harborne Primary School, Harborne

A Fairy's Flight

In the hush of dusk, 'neath stars so bright,
Fairies dance in the soft twilight,
Their wings aglow, they gently soar,
In the child's mind, for evermore.

Through clouds of silver they gracefully glide,
In the boundless sky, they beautifully ride,
Guiding dreams through the endless night,
Flying fairies, a mesmerising sight.

With each flap, a tale unfolds,
In the child's heart, their story holds,
In whispered breezes, their voices sing,
Of enchanted forests and eternal spring.

So let them soar in dreams so sweet,
Where flying fairies and magic meet,
In the child's world, they'll always play,
Wings of wonder, lighting the way.

Hiranya Nukala (11)
Harborne Primary School, Harborne

The Cave

What if there was a cave
At the end of the world,
Where evil things lay,
and thick mists swirled?

Axes tower in the corners,
Waiting for the use of the Grim Reaper.
Loud howls from the dead scream, "Keep her, keep her."

A girl that's trapped behind bars, waiting,
The man of death appears,
But it won't be long until (with the girl) he disappears.

I long to be woken
And be told it's just a dream,
But no one's there to help.
I feel a tap on my shoulder,
I wake up and give a yelp.

It's just my mum and I'm back in bed,
Not in that manky old cave.

Charlotte James (11)
Harborne Primary School, Harborne

My School, My Pride

My school… my pride!
Where we have a wonderful school ride.
We read, we write
And make our future bright!
We learn to respect,
Not to neglect.
We learn to accept,
Not to expect!
We play, we study,
With our best buddy!
Respect elders, obey parents,
Become sincere and punctual.
This is the habit we learn,
And that is why we call
My school, my pride.

Aya Agha (10)
Harborne Primary School, Harborne

A Dream

Lying **D** own on the bed, started
R eading until I said, maybe
E ight or even nine, after
A while I thought it was time. At
M idnight, I fell sound asleep, I
S tarted to hear noises and a little squeak.

Aarna Bhargava (11)
Harborne Primary School, Harborne

Dreams

D estinies
R eality left behind
E xciting adventures
A world of pure imagination
M any tomorrows
S o dive into the magical world of dreams and embrace it.

Soujanya Shanmugam (11)
Harborne Primary School, Harborne

Nightmares

I find myself in a land of horror and fright
I come to this place in my dreams once a night.
Creepy spiders scuttle around me, I begin to get afraid
I see spooky creatures hiding in the shade.
I need to get this out of my head, aimlessly I wonder
I spot something in the corner of my eye, is that the Loch Ness monster?
I hear the cackling of witches ringing in my ears
Suddenly before me, a terrible beast appears!
It lunges towards me, I try to run away
Although a herd of terrifying zombies are blocking my way!
Nowhere to run, I scream loudly in dread
I wake up to find myself in the comfort of my bed!
But these nightmares never leave me, forever they will keep,
Visiting me in my dreams when I close my eyes to sleep.

Finlay Torrington (10)
Highcliffe St Mark Primary School, Highcliffe

A Night In My Dreams

As I fall into a slumber,
I hear a noise that sounds like thunder.
It is the sound of a thousand magical hooves,
Coming to whisk me away, out of my shoes.

Soaring through the puffy clouds,
I let out a delighted yell out loud.
We land in the lush flowers, the colour of butter,
Where jackalopes hop and fairies flutter.

I hunt with the griffin down to the shore,
And the mermaids swim up from the sea floor.
They giggle and splash me and beckon me in,
But I climb upon my beautiful griffin.

We spend the day exploring and soaring
But soon we see with horror, the light is drawing.
The griffin goes still and ice-cold,
It's time for me to be brave and bold.

As I chase through the wood, the last of the light,
The creatures start forming out of the night.
Then I see the thickset coyote pull out his flute,
To hear its haunting music from its snoot.

When the last of the light goes with a pop,
The creatures circle, close in, they do not stop.
So when I dread that all is lost,
I hear the bark of the Kitsun's fox.

As I clutch to the fox's fur,
I hear the creature's defining purr.
"Go!" I scream with all my might,
As the creature tries to take a bite.

But too late! Kitsun has delivered me home,
I'll be back by tomorrow, that I do know.

Alba Mussell (9)
Highcliffe St Mark Primary School, Highcliffe

My Amazing Dream

I had a dream last night,
That I was on a flight.
We were going to Spain,
But I forgot my suitcase again.
We got to the house, it had a pool,
But my swimsuit was in my suitcase so I couldn't go at all.
Suddenly I was on a rocket going into space,
I got to the moon and had an alien race.
I jumped really high and almost touched the stars,
If I jumped any higher I could have reached Mars.
Suddenly a comet was taking me home,
It travelled faster than I'd ever known.
Flying over rooftops, it was really quite mad,
Then I opened my eyes and saw my dad.
He said we were late, I said what do you mean?
Then I remembered my amazing dream.

Erin Lowe (9)
Highcliffe St Mark Primary School, Highcliffe

My Dream Poem

Look at that lovely chocolate cake,
With shiny icing and a Flake,
The strawberry one is tempting too,
There's one for me and one for you,
I know you like the lemon one,
And I quite fancy that raspberry bun,
What a lovely time we had,
We ate the lot and felt so bad,
We couldn't have eaten any more,
We moaned and groaned, our tummies sore,
The daylight brushed across my eyes,
I tossed and turned and to my surprise,
I awoke from a dream,
It was a new day,
I won't be eating any cakes today!

Holly-Fay Middleton-Moore (10)
Highcliffe St Mark Primary School, Highcliffe

The Football Champions

F or some reason all I can dream about is football
O ne particular dream is stuck in my head
O n that day, my football team beat the best team in the league
T hat night I was so tired that I fell asleep really fast
B efore I knew it I was in my dream, being paraded around town with my team like champions
A ll the town were cheering for us
L oads of confetti was being fired out of cannons just for us
L et's hope one day this happens in real life

Bobby Blow (10)
Highcliffe St Mark Primary School, Highcliffe

At The Bottom Of My Garden

At the bottom of my garden
There's a badger and a fox
And lots of birds living
In the bird box

There's a family of woodlice
And a baby snail
Ants and butterflies
Are also on my nature trail

At the bottom of my garden
There's a squirrel and a bunny
And lots of slugs wriggling
Under the garden shed

Lots of cats and rats visit
But only on a Thursday do I see a bat
Not for long though
Perhaps next time I can record it

Lexie Fidler (10)
Highcliffe St Mark Primary School, Highcliffe

Fairy Magic

Once upon a dream,
I was skipping all alone,
In a meadow filled with flowers,
Then I saw a fairy home.

Out came a fairy,
As pink as can be,
Fluttering her fairy wings,
She put a spell on me.

A pair of wings grew on my back,
I gave them a little try,
Soon, before I knew it,
I was flying in the sky.

Another fairy came out of a door,
A shimmering gold, do you see?
With a wave of her magic hand,
She granted one more wish to me.

Jasmine Jackson (10)
Highcliffe St Mark Primary School, Highcliffe

Mum

When I go to bed at night,
I take off on an awesome flight.
To a world in the cupboard door,
Two points for Mum, if you're keeping score.

At night inside the cupboard door,
Chicken nuggets dance galore.
Salt and pepper do the tango,
Brussels sprouts and that cute little mango!

But cute little mango is feeling glum,
He's been picked on by that nasty chewing gum.
Yes he may be nice to chew,
But in my dreams, he's nasty too.

Lola Watson (10)
Highcliffe St Mark Primary School, Highcliffe

Once Upon A Dream

I dream of the sea and the treasures it brings,
The shells that get washed up and the ones that cling.
I dream of the sea and the crashing waves,
That pull all the sand and pebbles away.
I dream of the sea and the visits I have,
Making sandcastles and eating ice cream with my grandad.
I dream of the sea and the boats that pass by,
With the bright-coloured sails that catch my eye.
I dream of the sea,
And it's always a fun place to be!

Imogen Pengelly (9)
Highcliffe St Mark Primary School, Highcliffe

What Are Nightmares?

Nightmares could be creepy clowns,
The ones with manic, toothless frowns,
Or maybe giant, fat, hairy spiders,
The type you escape from on gliders.

Moaning, groaning, all they do,
Oh gosh, there's a zombie in my loo!
Get me out, I'm in the sea, surrounded by bloodthirsty piranhas,
Ouch! They're nipping my fluffy pyjamas.

I wake up full of dread,
Until I figure out I'm in my bed.

Phoebe Holdsworth (9)
Highcliffe St Mark Primary School, Highcliffe

The Monsters' End

In my dreams, I have been to this place.
I see these evil creatures that would bring fear to your face.
In this enchanted forest, these beasts are taking over.
I must save me and my friends before they get any closer.
Then, I prepare myself with courage and wisdom.
I promise to slay these beasts, that is my mission.
Now, the adventure goes on until the beasts are down.
Now I stand proud for the beasts have gone down!

Jake Moxom (9)
Highcliffe St Mark Primary School, Highcliffe

My Sports Day Last Year

A race track ahead.
T he crowd's anticipation spread.
H earts are racing and full of dread.
L ots of thoughts running through my head.
E xcitement with the steps I'm about to tread.
T he starter, "On your marks," he said.
E veryone pounding down the track and way in front I sped.
S tretching for the finish line I trip and bang my head.

Evie Bellamy (9)
Highcliffe St Mark Primary School, Highcliffe

Dreamland

D o dreams come true?
R eally hope they do.
E very magical land I go to when I close my eyes,
A mazing lights cover the sky.
M asters in the dark land, battle aliens in space,
L adies in beautiful gowns made of silk and lace.
A lways different every night,
N ever boring, always right.
D o dreams really come true? I really hope they do.

Emily Edwards (9)
Highcliffe St Mark Primary School, Highcliffe

Dancers

In my dreams I could see dancers that flew up high in the sky.
I was in a big stadium that flies in the sky.
I was in my seat when two big ugly teachers started to destroy everything.
Until my parents and friends saw them they started to freak out.
When they freaked out I hid under my seat.
As I was hiding under the big smelly seat I noticed something strange.
I was in a nightmare.

Grace Head (9)
Highcliffe St Mark Primary School, Highcliffe

Dream

Did I have the best dream last night?
I remember thinking I have to remember with all my might,
I remember there were lights so bright,
Where was I? I had to hold on tight,
Could it be real? Bright stars glowed up high,
There was a space coaster in my sights,
I was there, but do I remember why?
I'm not sure why, so I sigh,
I will have to try again next time.

Jake Waldron (9)
Highcliffe St Mark Primary School, Highcliffe

Untitled

I dream of my holiday in the sun
With all my family having fun!
Building sandcastles and eating ice creams
Oh, what a dream!
Swimming in the sea, what do I see?
A blue dolphin splashing next to me
He was jumping and splashing through the waves
Showing me tricks, I was so amazed
It was such a lovely holiday
Hopefully I can come back another day.

Lydia Pengelly (9)
Highcliffe St Mark Primary School, Highcliffe

Space Dreams

As I float in space,
I think, what is this place?

As I see my planet,
I begin to panic.

Am I dreaming in bed,
Or should I be screaming instead?

I can't remember,
It's dark and cold, is it December?

As I hear my alarm,
I finally become calm.

Phew, it was a dream,
Thank god, I scream!

Charlie Jarvis (9)
Highcliffe St Mark Primary School, Highcliffe

Dreams

Dreams can be long or short,
They can be exciting or dull,
They can be about pirates, bots or the sun,
They can be in bed on a plane or in the car,
Dreams are complex some are cool,
Some you can remember,
Some you cannot at all,
So treasure every one you have,
Some you like and some you don't,
Dreams are wonderful.

Henry Findlay (10)
Highcliffe St Mark Primary School, Highcliffe

Thailand

I'm dreaming about Thailand,
The hotel is very grand,
I'm feeling happy,
My new swim shorts look snappy,
I love jumping in the pool,
Swimming with my family is cool,
Old boats float on the water,
They make more noise than they ought to.

Riley Parker-Tait (10)
Highcliffe St Mark Primary School, Highcliffe

My Sandcastle

I made a sandcastle on the beach,
I used lots of sand,
I decorated it with seashells,
It was the prettiest,
It took me all day to make it perfect,
It really was hard work,
Along came a wave and washed it all away.

Samuel Watts (10)
Highcliffe St Mark Primary School, Highcliffe

Midnight Dreams

One clear night when stars glow bright,
I lie in bed as dreams come into my head.
Some are good, some are bad,
Some are happy, some are sad.
I open my eyes and to my surprise,
It was just a dream?

Megan Lammers (9)
Highcliffe St Mark Primary School, Highcliffe

Cotton Candy Cloud World

In my bed, I fall asleep,
I open my eyes and I think I'm awake, so I leap,
But I am actually in a world of dreams,
I look up and see a rubber duck and it is a light beam.
In a world of dreams, you would expect clouds,
But instead, there is cotton candy,
I find myself with Mummy and Daddy,
On a relaxing roller coaster that is speedy,
I get off the roller coaster,
I get my bottle out and notice the water inside is chocolate,
Flying around, I see another roller coaster but I feel ready,
To return to my warm and cosy bed,
A smile fills my face,
As Cotton Candy World plops into my head.

Joshua Millbrow (8)
Hormead CE School, Great Hormead

The Missing Object

I am a singing fairy in a band,
I flutter my wings,
As I sing,
I am happy as I am

But one day a goblin came,
And wanted all the fame,
He stole my magic microphone,
Leaving me alone,
Making me all sad.

The goblin in his haste,
Started picking up his pace,
He tripped and fell,
On some gel,
And the magic returned to me.

Now I'm happy as can be,
With a show for you all to see.

Erin Laidler (8)
Hormead CE School, Great Hormead

Dancer And Ed Sheeran

Once I had a dream,
Niamh and Ed Sheeran,
We were eating ice cream,
She wanted to dance,
And then had a chance,
To dance the night away,
Niamh wanted Ed Sheeran to stay,
It was a starry night,
And it was very bright.

Niamh Hennessey (8)
Hormead CE School, Great Hormead

The Midnight Kidnapper

One night, I got snatched from my bed while I was dreaming,
I woke up and saw a menacing pirate, glaring and scheming.
I was going to let out a shout,
But nothing came out.
I was about to get up and run away,
But the pirate gave me an urge to sit down and stay.

Luckily, then, the pirate went to go and use the bathroom,
I thought it was my chance as I tiptoed to the staffroom.
Although then, unexpectedly, I saw a white glowing eye,
I got closer and realised it was a camera they used to spy.

Suddenly I was cornered by a guy who looked like the captain,
As quickly as I could, I aimed at his face and threw a dirty napkin.
Then, as quick as a flash, I started sprinting north,
Although it seemed as if they were going back and forth.

Then a guy came at me with a stone sword,
And what looked like a shield made out of a wooden board.
Suddenly, I turned around and a pirate gave me a mean look,
But I threw a stone at him and that's all it took.
But then I saw the light, I thought for sure I was dead,
Suddenly I heard a voice saying, "Wake up! You're late for school, get out of bed!"

Ben Skinsley (9)
James Cambell Primary School, Dagenham

Lollie Pop In The Olympics

Lollie Pop in the Olympics,
Swinging from bar to bar,
She's doing amazing, but won't get so far.

I believe Lollie Pop will win with a passion,
And her gymnastics uniform is such a fashion,
More people are coming in,
While sweat is dropping from her skin.

The Olympics may begin!
I thought they were going to call her name,
But instead, she ends up losing her game!
What a shame,
She is getting replaced,
They should give her a chance to start her dance.

But then there is a plot twist,
If she was last on the list,
There was time to make a change,
But Lollie looked really sad,
If I don't make a change this will be bad.

That was when the Ice Cream came,
So Lollie could be saved,
We better be fast, but not possible,
We tried at last.

Teagan Rema (9)
James Cambell Primary School, Dagenham

The Boy And The Child

See the running of the adolescent,
I think he is angry at the pre-adolescent.

He finds it hard to see the lake,
Overshadowed by the content coral snake.

Who is that sleeping near the cheese?
I think she'd like to eat overseas.

She is but an awful child,
Admired as she sits upon a little child

Her exciting car is just a lorry,
It needs no gas, it runs on territory.

She's not alone, she brings a queen,
A pet skunk and lots of hygiene.

The skunk likes to chase a pepper,
Especially one that's in a klepper.

The adolescent shudders at the sharp ghosts,
He wants to leave, but she wants the cinnamon toast.

Ivan Al-Wakeel (10)
James Cambell Primary School, Dagenham

My Dreams At Night!

    D iving into the deep warm sky
    R eading the stars
h **E** aring the outer world
    A nd with a warm welcome
    M y brain starts to depart
    S aying, "Oh, what a wonderful time it is"

A nd
R eaching out to the sky
E ven not a single fly

A n opening sign
L owering me lower and lower
L ooking down

I can feel the warm breeze passing by

K nowing it's all for me
N ever fighting by
O pen my hands and say
W hat a wonderful time it was.

Gabi Dumitrescu (10)
James Cambell Primary School, Dagenham

The Classroom At Night

At night, I saw the classroom,
Dancing,
Book front-flipped off the bookshelf,
The chairs spun in the bright moonlight.

At night, I saw the classroom,
Singing,
Tables put on a show for the chairs,
Pencils danced on the page whilst singing their hearts out,
The sunshine cushion dazzled as if on BGT.

At night, I saw the classroom,
Eating,
Dictionaries munched on words,
Thesauruses burped so loud the other side of the world heard,
The bins were gagging because of how much they ate,
The sofa was spitting out the cushion fluff.

Freya Ellis (10)
James Cambell Primary School, Dagenham

Last Night I Saw The Classroom

Last night, I saw the classroom still,
Chairs tucked in,
Blinds closed, shut,
Pencils still, like a rock.

Last night, I saw the classroom moving,
People tucking their chairs before leaving for home,
Blinds still opened,
The computer, still not powered off.

Last night, I saw the classroom happy,
Nobody was sick,
They were all happy,
Pencils dance through the paper gracefully,
They played games the whole afternoon.

Last night, I saw the classroom sad,
Nobody there,
No seats,
The classroom was sad.

Aka Onuorah (10)
James Cambell Primary School, Dagenham

The Dimension Of A Future

The world is full of history,
But there is lots of mystery,
I wish I could leave at night
And see the city, an amazing sight,
I turned on the light,
Without any fright,
Then I pulled up my sleeve,
And went to leave,
And thought it right
To enjoy the night,
I reached the city at dawn,
And had a bunch of yawns,
Children were sent to school,
Parents were ready to cool,
Breakfast clubs are making well best comes,
Parents are murmuring about what to eat,
While poor toddlers are left on the seat.

Mehroz Riaz (9)
James Cambell Primary School, Dagenham

It Was Just A Dream

One dark night I woke up at midnight,
I knew it was just an ordinary night,
I was wishing for toys to come alive,
And fell asleep again.

One spooky night, I woke up again,
But this time, I saw a wizard wink at me,
Then he clicked magically,
And all my toys came to life!

I saw them move, play and talk,
I rushed to them to play with them,
But in five minutes, I went back to sleep,
And realised it was just a dream.

Artiom Pozdirea (10)
James Cambell Primary School, Dagenham

What Happens In The Sky

I wake up to an annoying sound,
When I realise I'm above the ground,
I look around,
No one to be found,
I am as single as a Pringle,
My bedsheet starts to wrinkle,
As dragons fight with passion,
And unicorns fight with action,
Wizards play with lizards,
Fairies play with canaries,
This is too weird for me,
I must get out of this nonsense!

Gabriele Stravinskaite (9)
James Cambell Primary School, Dagenham

Hit It In

Dance beneath the stars,
As I twirl away in the night,
I let the thunder overtake me,
As lightning fills the sky,
Then I feel the force of nature,
Penetrate my skin as magic sinks in,
That's when I realise,
That even backward steps,
Are part of a dance.

Michelle Oloko (9)
James Cambell Primary School, Dagenham

The Three Odd Lambs

Once upon a dream,
There was an old sheep
Trying to give birth to KitKat Peep.
In a giant barn in Sweden,
A lamb as pink as Barbie's car popped out,
It was KitKat Peep's brother, Digestive Peep.
Then another, this one was green like grass.
This one was Hobnob Peep
And then finally a red lamb popped out onto the hard ground,
This lamb was red like The Flash.
It tried to stand but instead of standing it floated in the air.
Then the green one tried to stand up,
It started talking to me,
It said, "Hello, my name is Hobnob Peep,
I am a cow.
Then finally the pink one tried,
She started zooming round the pen.

Alfie Marr (10)
Kirkinner Primary School, Kirkinner

The Snowy White Horse

Once upon a dream,
There was a gigantic snowy white horse named Steam.
He galloped right down to my feet shaking his head
And kicking his feet.
I jumped on his back and galloped up the lane
To see the king and tell him my name.
He said hello and I said neigh.
He jumped up and down, spun all around
Just to have a kind friend.

Lily McShane
Kirkinner Primary School, Kirkinner

The Mouse And The Bear

Once upon a dream,
There was a grumpy blue bear called Gleam.
He liked sleeping on a chair, that was green.
He saw a red mouse in yellow underwear,
That looked fiery and mean.
The mouse was climbing up a ladder to get all the cream.
Suddenly he fell. *Bang*, he hurt his spleen.
Thankfully it was just a dream!

Leyla McQueen (10)
Kirkinner Primary School, Kirkinner

Poor Princess

P oor princess
R ight under the bed
I n the castle it was a ginormous room that was red
N ow she's on the red bed
C ooking a plan in her head
E vil witch created a
S pell to vanish the princess
S top, it will never work!

Carter Hastie (10)
Kirkinner Primary School, Kirkinner

The Puppies

Once upon a dream,
There was a dog having little puppies
And one of the puppies was as gold as the Olympic Rings!
And also had superhuman strength and speed!
The storm brewed and made a big crash!
Then the puppies ran in a dash!
They got to safety and had a rash.

Georgie Doherty (8)
Kirkinner Primary School, Kirkinner

The Abandoned Pencil

I am a wooden pencil,
Broken in half.
Left on the floor,
Lonely and cold.

Jay Chauhan (8)
Lawn Primary School, Allestree

Once Upon A Dream

I am sitting on a cloud and looking at what's above me.
I see a beautiful sunset with fairies dancing and unicorns' horns shimmering.
I see the bright yellow sun blooming in the sky.
I see a marvellous rainbow,
And on the rainbow there is a glittery emerald,
Sparkles all glooming the sky with glitter.
When you step on the sunset you think bright thoughts,
And whatever you wish for comes true.
Did you know, even if it is not night, fireworks are popping in the air?
When you see these fireworks,
Your eyes are amazed and your jaw falls in amazement.
In your head you are thinking, *wow these fireworks are the best.*
I've never seen any type of firework like these before.

Shahmeen Jalil (8)
Parsloes Primary School, Dagenham

Shooting Star

Oh, the dream I had it was magnificent really.
Come into the light and see it all bright.
I sit on the moon and stare at the sky.
Every night I have this dream,
Oh I just wish it was real.
Just one glimpse of these pictures,
And you will fall in love with the fascinating colours,
And best of all, the shooting star.
The colours mix with gold and silver.
The stars twinkle with every second,
The moment you gaze your life is just a cloud in the sky.
This shooting star brightens it all as I drink a warm, cosy hot chocolate,
It makes me feel at home.
I gaze for hours, how could you ever get bored of such a sight?
This dream is just what you need.

Fatima Zubair (9)
Parsloes Primary School, Dagenham

The Unicorn Fantasy

In my special dream, unicorns flew
And sparkled below,
The wind blew,
And the ocean glowed.
The sky was blue and the grass was green,
Growing beneath,
The trees danced
And a fox glanced.
The baker made a pack of cookies
As I explored this fantasy,
I said, "Oh, what a beauty
With all these little cuties!"
I flew in the clouds
And watched the little kids play in the park.
I woke up,
I thought it was my real world,
But it was all in my fantasy.

Daria Onila (9)
Parsloes Primary School, Dagenham

Unicorns

U p high in the sky, unicorns were flying high,
N othing else was there except for me,
I was wearing a crown on my head, was I the queen?
C orn was my best friend, she loved playing with me!
O n my back were sparkling wings, how didn't I notice this?
R unning and playing were their favourite things to do
N ow it was getting dark and the sunset was amazing!
S uddenly I woke up, it was just a wonderful dream.

Ella Avram (9)
Parsloes Primary School, Dagenham

My Dream

Monday through to Friday,
I have to go to school,
My teacher is a lady,
I think she's really cool.

Some days I can be naughty,
And friends don't want to play,
I have to stop and listen,
To what the adults say.

I'm trying not to be that boy,
So help me if you can,
Then I will help you as I grow,
And be a better man.

Then, I woke up.

Owen Clavier (9)
Parsloes Primary School, Dagenham

Swirling And Tumbling

Once I close my eyes, I dream about a giant orange spider crawling up my arm.
It feels ticklish.
I sit up and then a flying car swirls around my head like a tornado.
The car speaks and I jump inside.
We fly to the moon, as fast as a train.
The moon cracks and I begin to fall.
Swirling and tumbling, around and around.
I land by a toy shop.
So many things to see.
I don't know what to buy.
Then I opened my eyes and I knew it was all a dream.

Mabel Hatt (8)
Pencombe CE Primary School, Pencombe

The War Of The Elements!

The sun, raging for revenge,
As balls of fire hit the land.
People watch while it sets the world on fire,
Burning all the houses to ashes!
All the elements start to get angry,
It sounds like a war.
Air soars down from high above the clouds,
Water swims up to shore,
Arising from the secret depths of the ocean,
Earth awakens and stomps away, coming from the underworld.
Air blows a gust of wind towards the raging fire,
Nothing happens except the fire spreads.
Air now knows that his power won't help.
Earth tries to flatten the flames
But the flames just jump on the rocks and devour them into ashes.
His iron will just go through the flames but it won't melt
Sand can put the fire out.
But it won't do it all,
It's down to Water,
He knows what he can do!

Waves crash on the world and wipe the fire out.
All the flames vanish,
But the glowing sun is still angry,
The four elements glide up to space in their magical suits.
They present the sun with a gift.
A phoenix springs out and swirls around the sun
The sun now gets a fiery friend who can calm him down and keep the sun company.
The sun will never hurt the world again!
Everything is now peaceful.

Sophia Ashby (8)
Ramsbury Primary School, Ramsbury

The Banana In The Limo

I had a dream I owned a limo,
Inside it, there was a pillow.
It was there for me to rest,
So I was on my banana quest.

The driver was a marshmallow
Named Rick, but he was not a fellow,
He would not pick the engine, pick the pedal,
Pick them both, he played the cello.
I asked for some music and he played the ABCs,
So I said, "Oh, please!"

I was hungry, so I went to a shop,
I bought human arms, it was for the top.
I went back in the limo but it was not only me,
It was a muffin, with a beard you see.

And then I realised it was not a dream,
It was me, the banana, as fun as can be!

Charlotte Pontoppidan-Toms (10)
Ramsbury Primary School, Ramsbury

Wolf Dogs

In my dreams I have the moon's light,
With floating wolf dogs shining bright.
Some are black and some are pink,
Some are green with an orange tinge.
When I see them pass by me,
It makes me wonder, wonder with glee!
Every night I give them bones,
With the hope they might not go.
But never have I had such luck,
I always just keep getting stuck.
And every time they just disappear,
They leave me lost until next year.

Abi Fellows (9)
Ramsbury Primary School, Ramsbury

Spells With Squishmallows

S quishmallows of magic, what a surprise
P articular weirdness in front of my eyes
E ager to learn, though my stomach may churn
L evitating objects above the ground
L eather robes, wooden wands, and things which were not meant to be found
S adly, when I open my eyes, my head will stop telling these magical lies.

Lorcan Cooper (10)
Ramsbury Primary School, Ramsbury

The Witching Hour

In the inky sky at night,
A glowing haze will give you a fright.
She hovers up in the misty sky,
A wicked phantom flies so high.
Waiting for midnight to strike,
We know there will be trouble tonight.
Deep in the darkest witching hour,
Into our dreams she comes with her full power.
Wake up.

Izzy Gray (8)
Ramsbury Primary School, Ramsbury

Camping In Wales

In my dreams, the Welsh dunes move,
A warm evening swim really soothes,
A barbecue cooks while we kids play,
Straight to sleep after a lovely day,
When the sand is very hot,
We run, jump, skip and hop,
We find a swing in a tree,
I'm so happy being me.

Alex Soper (8)
Ramsbury Primary School, Ramsbury

Emma Whatwood

I once knew a girl called Emma,
Or Emma Whatwood shall I say,
Whatever Emma said was a "What?" or a "Yay!"
In the night she dreams of forests,
And wonders where they are by day!

Iris Fawcus (9)
Ramsbury Primary School, Ramsbury

I Dream

You may insult, punch and shove me
With your horrible, twisted lies
You may drown me but
Like a phoenix so bright, I dream

Just like the Northern Lights shining
With the certainty of the beautiful skies
Just like dreams in the night

Departing behind weeks of trauma and rain, I rise
Embracing a new day that leaves behind the anxiety I dream
I am the dream that shines the truth
From my mother who gave me my youth
I dream, I rise, I dream,

Quote: Follow your dreams and your passions and life will guide you through the right way.

Khaleelah Gbagba (9)
Rufford Primary & Nursery School, Bulwell

A Football Legend

F oot, you use your foot in football.
O nly use your foot when kicking and laying passes on the field.
O nly frequent practice can make you a professional footballer.
T ime to toss the ball around in the backyard with my sister.
B ig game comes after spending time practising with teammates.
A football pitch only allows team players to combine.
L ettuce is one of the healthy meals for professional footballers.
L egendary players must have good qualities to influence the next generation.

Victor Adebayo (8)
Rufford Primary & Nursery School, Bulwell

In A Dream I Can...

In a dream, I can walk on water,
Even though it's getting colder,
In a dream, I want to be an author,
But first I need to get older.

In a dream, I can go to school on a dragon,
Still, I want to buy a jeep wagon,
Football is my talent,
And a dragon could be a bit violent.

In a dream, I can be me,
In a dream, I want to be me,
In a dream, I'm allowed to be me,
And nothing can change that.

Jayden Lewis (9)
Rufford Primary & Nursery School, Bulwell

Bad Day!

Quick, quick, get out of the house,
Because there is a lot of mouse,
Here, there, almost everywhere,
We have to go outside!
No sign of a bus or train,
Not even a car to pick us up,
Because... it is raining!
Why is this happening to me?
Oh boy, it must be...
A bad day!

Georgia Sail (9)
Rufford Primary & Nursery School, Bulwell

Join The Beat

M is for movement, I want to see you dance
U is for utopia, I'll send you into a trance
S is for sound, listen to the beat of my track
I is me, I'm DJ Yes Jack
C is for career, this is where I want to go, moving people around the world, solo.

Jack Boardman (9)
Rufford Primary & Nursery School, Bulwell

Join In With Art

A fantastic thing to do when you're bored,
Really fun to do with other people,
Totally fun for anyone.

Brayden Chadwick (8)
Rufford Primary & Nursery School, Bulwell

Dreams

As the wondrous animals scattered on the grassy lands,
They followed through the wavy paths,
As the night turned to day,
They would think they have gone astray.

When they fell asleep, they loved to dream and dream,
There was a horse that spread out her wings,
The horse flew high in the sky.

As the leaves turned green and the sky blue,
Go out for a ride, just me and you.
Day turned to night, from the fright.
Look at the stars, they glide our way
Because soon the whole world will speak of our name.
Go to sleep now, dream and dream,
Smell the wondrous scent of a feather,
Look up to the beautiful weather.
Rainbow scattered on the sparkling sky
And flight that can be high!

Henon Yosef (10)
Sacred Heart RC Primary School, Birchfield

Nevertheless A Dream

All alone in the dark of night,
Not going down without a fight.
In the void and the magical dust,
Beneath my feet I can feel the crust.
I feel scared, I look afar, I see a creature,
I scrub my eyes as if it's a feature,
It chases and I run,
It's as if this is fun,
I see a bright light, I go towards it,
It's as if a candle just got lit,
With lots of buildings and people
It's as if I am feeble,
The next thing I see a man,
He said he was a fan,
A fan of my beauty, he said I should be on the stage,
I am on stage and it's a faith,
I am now famous,
I hope people are not jealous.

Emmanuella Chinedu (10)
Sacred Heart RC Primary School, Birchfield

Myths, Myths

Myths, myths what shall we pick?
The one with the boy and Zeus?
Is this the one we should choose?
Up above the clouds, above the world,
Lies lonely Zeus.
Down on land lying in bed is a lowly boy waiting for freedom.
Alone, lost in a garden of flowers,
Lying down, hopeless, not knowing where to go,
Him thinking nothing has been prepared for him
As this strange land he sees,
Anxiety crawls around his face,
As the night sky darkens, the big hole in his chest widens,
Zeus awakens, there is nothing to escape him again.

Tanjima Hassain (10)
Sacred Heart RC Primary School, Birchfield

Enchanted World

No way home,
The wind sways alone,
The fairies flitter
And show me glitter.
The wizards' noses are lumpy,
And always grumpy.
Hi, me Tae, I walk around every day
In the enchanted forest,
A princess, no access in a castle,
The princess is cold,
And I know not to be told!
How rude,
I always think about it when I snooze,
The code was put, behead the toad.
The princess nice and warm,
No more storms,
No more screams in her dreams,
Safe and sound.

Tavia Morgan (10)
Sacred Heart RC Primary School, Birchfield

From Darkness Into The Light!

Out of sight,
Out of mind,
Into the deep,
Come out blind,
Reach for the darkness, see what you find,
Follow the light,
Leave it all behind,
At the end, I'm friends with light,
The light would not be afraid to shine,
Let the darkness lead you into the light,
Where the shadow's reach is out of sight,
To free you into the night,
Let the world fall into your hands,
Let the darkness empower your world.

Sarina Zegard (9)
Sacred Heart RC Primary School, Birchfield

Off To School

Blue ribbons in my hair,
Shoes wrapped in a bow on my feet,
The bag neatly laid till it's square,
Then the rain ruins my amazing uniform,
Suddenly my shoes were soaking,
Then my socks were drenched,
This weather is disgusting,
To be in England is really disgusting,
The environment and climate change.

Kha'mya Gayle
Sacred Heart RC Primary School, Birchfield

Unknown

As I was sleeping I saw a monster,
Green skin,
Sharp teeth, I couldn't believe it,
It came closer,
I couldn't bear but stare,
I froze,
I didn't know what to do,
I went to bed
And dozed,
Like nothing happened,
That morning he was gone,
Not even a bone.

Raphael Glorified (10)
Sacred Heart RC Primary School, Birchfield

Fairies

I woke up in the morning to a confused start,
Fairies lying round in sight,
It felt majestic as if it was true,
But there was a test due,
An adventure awaits,
Suddenly a quest awaits for us dearly,
Fairies of fire and fairies of shame.
Fairies of the healthy and of the lame.

Oluwaferanmi Ayandiran (9)
Sacred Heart RC Primary School, Birchfield

I Saw A Peacock

I saw a peacock with a fiery tail,
I saw a blazing comet drop down hail,
I saw a cloud with ivy circled around,
I saw a sturdy oak creep on the ground,
I saw a fish swallow up a whale,
I saw a raging sea brim full of ale.

Sarina Suha Zegard (10)
Sacred Heart RC Primary School, Birchfield

The Chasers

Sandcross School: Priority
The night the dream chasers fly is the best night of all,
As they swoop in and out of houses and roofs,
They call to each other, "Dream Chasers, dream!"
Now as they dive into my house,
I hear them land softly in my room,
When they sprinkle magic dust on me,
I hear them talking to one another,
"Let's fly through the aurora borealis tonight."
As they fly away,
I dream, of being a dream chaser.

Seren Walker-Samuel (7)
Sandcross School, Reigate

Cute Land Is The Place To Be

Once there was a world far, far away called Cute Land.
In Cute Land there was a cute clown and my toy kitten came alive!
Can you see?

And as we went along I jumped into the sea,
I discovered that when I jumped in the ocean,
I became a mermaid! It was magic not a potion.

"Wow," I said as I was swimming along the ocean
With my beautiful rainbow mermaid,
Oh my gosh, this is amazing,
I could not stop gazing.

I spotted some seaweed in the ocean and I found a big mermaid palace,
Inside there was a girl called Alice.
She was right in front of me and the huge doors opened by themselves.

I swam inside with my mermaid tail along behind me,
And guess who I saw there?
Sitting in a pink chair! Isadora Moon, Pink Rabbit and Emerald and Delphina,
Who were the most amazing things I've ever seen.

"Emerald and Delphina, Isadora and Pink Rabbit, why are you here?" I asked.
Isadora answered, "We are here because there's a party and we made a cake,
It's in the oven to bake."

"It's your birthday and you didn't even know! You're just a tiny bit late,
But I guess you couldn't wait!" said Emerald and Delphina nodded.

And they all sang, "Happy birthday to you, happy birthday to you,
Happy birthday to Elizabeth, happy birthday to you.
Happy 8th birthday, Elizabeth."
"Oh my gosh, this is the best birthday ever!
I hope it finishes never!"

After the party I went back up to Cute Land
And Delphina and Emerald went up too,
Both of them didn't have a clue.

They'd got legs as well, oh my gosh! They looked so posh.
I noticed that she didn't have a mermaid's tail anymore,
And she said, "Let's go buy some fruit at the store."

And we lived happily ever after in Cute Land.

Elizabeth Reeve (7)
Sandcross School, Reigate

Sunny And Molly's Sweet Adventure

S uddenly candy is appearing everywhere
W hilst the girls are asleep
E xcitedly they wake up, awoken by the smell
E verything is extreme, cotton candy, popping candy
T reats, goodies, all they have dreamt of
S ugary delight.

Amelia Marsh (7)
Sandcross School, Reigate

Dreams

Once you get in your bed
People rise from the dead.
Don't get scared,
It is all a dream,
So you're safe at home
In your beam.
Light up,
It's fine,
All safe in your bed.

Harry Rheinberg (8)
Sandcross School, Reigate

Sheep

S heep in my dreams
H ave lots of fun
E ach and every one has a different colour
E very one unique and different sizes
P ut them to bed and you'll have a good dream.

Connie Noble (8)
Sandcross School, Reigate

A Faraway Place Called Dreamland

Slowly drifting off, I close my eyes,
Hoping that in my dreams I find a surprise...

I'm in a land, so vast and wide,
That behind the trees I run to hide.
The soft lush grass tickles my toes,
And the smell of flowers enters my nose.
This isn't a nightmare, but a dream,
It's just not what it seems.

Through the trees I wander,
In my head I wonder,
But then, in the corner of my eye, I spot a boat,
Which bobs on a river, afloat,
I stroll to it, get in, and begin to row,
To another place, with people, and covered in snow.

Here, I see fairies, that gleam and glow,
And a princess with beautiful hair and a bow.
I get out of the boat and she welcomes me,
To this magical world, filled with happiness and glee!

Sheep

S heep in my dreams
H ave lots of fun
E ach and every one has a different colour
E very one unique and different sizes
P ut them to bed and you'll have a good dream.

Connie Noble (8)
Sandcross School, Reigate

A Faraway Place Called Dreamland

Slowly drifting off, I close my eyes,
Hoping that in my dreams I find a surprise...

I'm in a land, so vast and wide,
That behind the trees I run to hide.
The soft lush grass tickles my toes,
And the smell of flowers enters my nose.
This isn't a nightmare, but a dream,
It's just not what it seems.

Through the trees I wander,
In my head I wonder,
But then, in the corner of my eye, I spot a boat,
Which bobs on a river, afloat,
I stroll to it, get in, and begin to row,
To another place, with people, and covered in snow.

Here, I see fairies, that gleam and glow,
And a princess with beautiful hair and a bow.
I get out of the boat and she welcomes me,
To this magical world, filled with happiness and glee!

Suddenly, I'm being sucked away from this world,
And I find myself in bed, all curled.

I guess I visited a world I cannot understand,
A faraway place called Dreamland.

Kaila Kovalcik (10)
St James's RC Primary School, Twickenham

I Wish I Could Fly

In twilight's embrace, my heart takes flight,
Yearning to soar, through the veil of night.
Wings of dreams unfurl a celestial desire,
To dance with the stars, in the cosmic choir.

Oh, to traverse the azure expanse above,
Where whispers of freedom softly rove.
In daydreams I weave a tapestry of sky,
Wishing on breezes, with a heartfelt sigh.

Feathers of hope paint the canvas of my mind,
A symphony of flight, in the vast open bind.
To hug the clouds and chase the sun's embrace,
Oh, how I wish to fly in boundless grace.

Matthew Zuaiter Viono (11)
St James's RC Primary School, Twickenham

That Night

That night I crept out of bed,
Wishing no one ever knew.
And as I walked ahead,
Something glowed.
So then I followed it,
To the dark, gloomy forest.

I hid behind the bush, catching an eye on it,
A beautiful, bright blue creature with the shape of a reindeer.
It was the prettiest thing ever to exist,
But after a few minutes it disappeared.
I closed my eyes in exhaustion,
Suddenly I woke up and found out it was just a dream.

Kylie Lo (11)
St James's RC Primary School, Twickenham

Space

High up above in the sky so high
Lives life up there
No one ever knew where and never knew why
Any moment now it can disappear into thin air.

All the stars have different shapes and sizes
It all comes to life when the moon rises
Some small, some tall
Or even as hard as a brick wall

All galaxies and milky ways
Will all brighten up our gloomy days
Every planet like Earth or Saturn
They all somehow form a big pattern.

High up above in the sky so high
Lives life up there
No one ever knew where and never knew why
All the stars can fall out of your pocket
And venture into the sky.

Anna Kostyleva (9)
The Eveline Day School, Tooting

YOUNG WRITERS INFORMATION

We hope you have enjoyed reading this book – and that you will continue to in the coming years.

If you're a young writer who enjoys reading and creative writing, or the parent of an enthusiastic poet or story writer, do visit our website **www.youngwriters.co.uk**. Here you will find free competitions, workshops and games, as well as recommended reads, a poetry glossary and our blog.

If you would like to order further copies of this book, or any of our other titles, then please give us a call or visit **www.youngwriters.co.uk**.

Young Writers
Remus House
Coltsfoot Drive
Peterborough
PE2 9BF
(01733) 890066
info@youngwriters.co.uk

YoungWritersUK   **YoungWritersCW**
youngwriterscw   **youngwriterscw**